· De Colores ·

and Other Latin-American Folk Songs
for Children

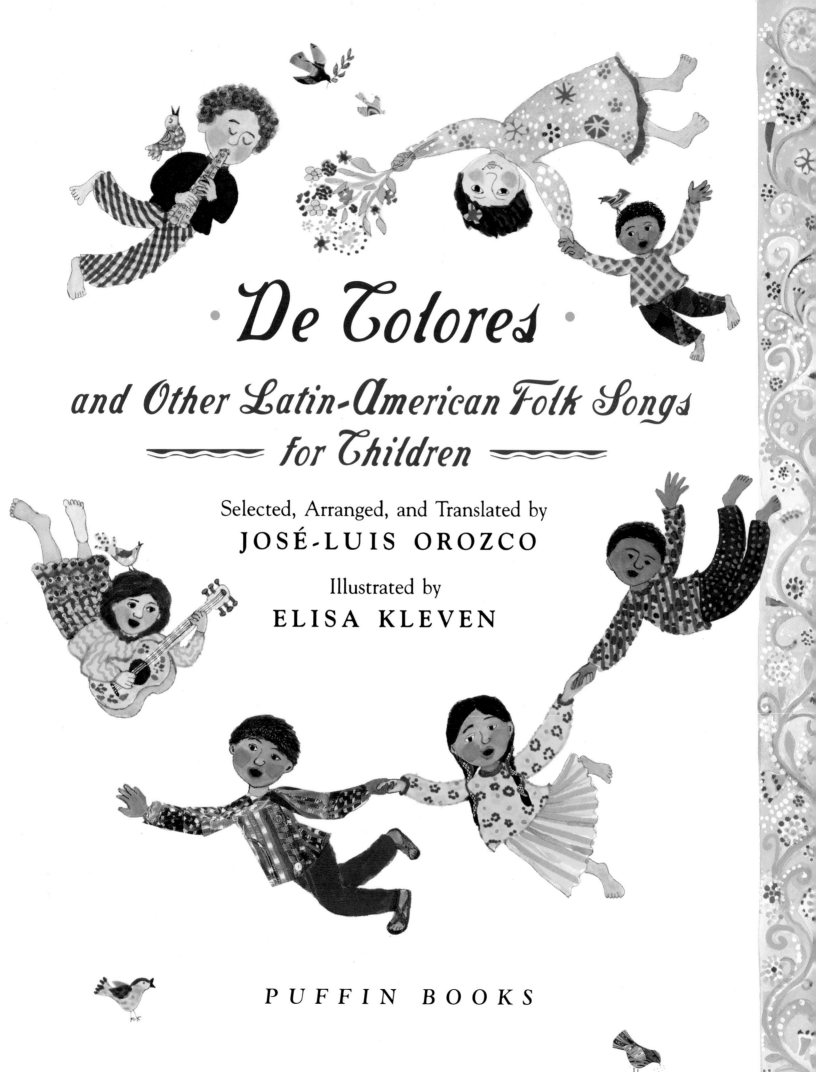

De Colores ·

and Other Latin-American Folk Songs
for Children

Selected, Arranged, and Translated by
JOSÉ-LUIS OROZCO

Illustrated by
ELISA KLEVEN

PUFFIN BOOKS

Para Julie, José-Luis, Maya, Gabriel y Pablito
J.-L.O.

For Sally and her music
E.K.

The illustrator would like to thank Carol Schneider,
Minerva Mendoza, and the Thomas family
for their generosity.

PUFFIN BOOKS
Published by the Penguin Group
Penguin Putnam Books for Young Readers, 345 Hudson Street, New York, New York 10014, U.S.A.
Penguin Books Ltd, 27 Wrights Lane, London W8 5TZ, England
Penguin Books Australia Ltd, Ringwood, Victoria, Australia
Penguin Books Canada Ltd, 10 Alcorn Avenue, Toronto, Ontario, Canada M4V 3B2
Penguin Books (N.Z.) Ltd, 182-190 Wairau Road, Auckland 10, New Zealand

Penguin Books Ltd, Registered Offices: Harmondsworth, Middlesex, England

First published in the United States of America by Dutton Children's Books, a division of Penguin Books USA Inc., 1994
Published by Puffin Books, a member of Penguin Putnam Books for Young Readers, 1999

22 23 24 25 26 27 28 29 30

Lyrics and music arrangements copyright © José-Luis Orozco, 1994
Illustrations copyright © Elisa Kleven, 1994
All rights reserved

CIP data is available.

Puffin Books ISBN 0-14-056548-5

Manufactured in China

The art in this book is mixed-media collage, using
watercolors, pastels, ink, and cut paper.

All of the songs contained in this book have been recorded
by José-Luis Orozco and are available from Arcoiris Records,
P.O. Box 7428, Berkeley, CA 94707

Preface

This rich collection of children's music from the Spanish-speaking world represents the contributions of many people from cultures in Europe, Africa, and the Americas who have handed down songs from one generation to the next—songs for special occasions and for every day, songs for learning, for singing in a family or group, and songs just for fun.

Many of these pieces I learned as a child from my grandmother, mother, or friends in the barrio of Peralvillo in Mexico City. Others I heard from the families with whom I lived as I traveled through North, Central, and South America, the Caribbean, and Spain during a three-year journey with the Mexico City Children's Choir. More recently, some have come from my frequent tours to Mexico and to Spanish-speaking communities in the United States. My work with children has also inspired me to write my own songs for them, two of which are included here. Although I have tried to preserve tradition as much as possible, I have, where appropriate, adapted lyrics and music in both Spanish and English to encourage enjoyment and participation.

I hope this collection strikes a chord with children and with those who work with children. Special thanks to all who help preserve this rich musical heritage so that our children of today may take pleasure in passing it on to the children of tomorrow.

Contents

Buenos días · Good Morning

This song exists in many different languages. The French version, "Frère Jacques," is probably the oldest. In Spanish it is found as "Martinillo," "Fray Felipe," and "Bartolito." This version, which emphasizes greetings and times of day, can be sung as a round; a person or group starts and is followed after the first line by a second group. Or it can be sung as call and response.

Buenos días, buenos días,	Good morning, good morning,
¿cómo estás? ¿cómo estás?	How are you? How are you?
Muy bien, gracias,	Very well, I thank you,
Muy bien, gracias,	Very well, I thank you,
¿y usted? ¿y usted?	How about you? How about you?
Buenas tardes, buenas tardes,	Good afternoon, good afternoon,
¿cómo estás? ¿cómo estás?	How are you? How are you?
Muy bien, gracias,	Very well, I thank you,
Muy bien, gracias,	Very well, I thank you,
¿y usted? ¿y usted?	How about you? How about you?
Buenas noches, buenas noches,	Good evening, good evening,
¿cómo estás? ¿cómo estás?	How are you? How are you?
Muy bien, gracias,	Very well, I thank you,
Muy bien, gracias,	Very well, I thank you,
¿y usted? ¿y usted?	How about you? How about you?

For call and response, a person or group sings the boldface words and a second person or group repeats.

Sing the days of the week in the same manner.

Hoy es lunes, hoy es lunes,   **Today is Monday,** *today is Monday,*
¿cómo estás? ¿cómo estás?   ***How are you?*** *How are you?*
mártes   *Tuesday*
miércoles   *Wednesday*
jueves   *Thursday*
viernes   *Friday*
sábado   *Saturday*
domingo   *Sunday*

El chocolate · The Chocolate

The drink of the cocoa bean—chocolate—is a gift to the world from Mexico and Central America. The word comes from the Nahuatl language, in which xoco-atl means "bitter water" and cacahuatl-atl means "cacao water." The song can be sung as call and response, with the leader singing each line and the group repeating it. Children can also sing the song faster and faster, and they can rub their hands together in imitation of the molinillo, or chocolate stirrer.

U-no, dos, tres, | CHO, u-no, dos, tres, | CO, u-no, dos, tres, | LA, u-no, dos, tres,

TE, u-no, dos, tres, | TE, cho-co-la-te, cho-co-la-te, ba-te, ba-te el cho-co-

la-te, cho-co-la-te, cho-co-la-te, ba-te, ba-te el cho-co-la-te.

Uno, dos, tres, CHO,
uno, dos, tres, CO,
uno, dos, tres, LA,
uno, dos, tres, TE...

chocolate, chocolate,
bate, bate el chocolate.

[cantar dos veces]

One, two, three, CHO,
one, two, three, CO,
one, two, three, LA,
one, two, three, TE...

chocolate, chocolate,
beat and beat the chocolate.

[sing twice]

El barquito · The Little Boat

Here's an amusing song. It has no end. As you sing it, count the number of weeks on your fingers. This version comes from Paraguay.

Ha - bía u - na vez un bar - co chi - qui - to, ha - bía u - na

vez un bar - co - chi - qui to, ha - bía u - na

vez un bar - co chi - qui - to, tan chi - qui - to, tan chi -

qui - to, que no po - día na - ve - gar. Pa - sa - ron u - na, dos, tres, cua - tro, cin - co, seis, sie - te se - ma - nas,

Había una vez
un barco chiquito,   [cantar tres veces]
tan chiquito, tan chiquito,
que no podía navegar.

Pasaron una, dos, tres, cuatro,
cinco, seis, siete semanas,   [cantar tres veces]
y el barquito tan chiquito
que no podía navegar.

Y si la historia no les
parece larga,   [cantar tres veces]
volveremos, volveremos,
volveremos a empezar.

Había una vez…

Oh! once there was
a very little boat   [sing three times]
that was tiny, was so tiny,
that it couldn't sail away.

We counted one and two, three and four,
five and six and seven weeks more,   [sing three times]
and the tiny boat was so tiny
that it couldn't sail away.

And if you think that the
story has an end,   [sing three times]
we are ready, we are ready
to start all over again.

Oh! once there was…

Al tambor · The Drum Song

This song is sung in Panama during carnaval and at other celebrations. The original rhythm is called *tamborcito* and the people of the country are honored: "Panameña, panameña, panameña, vida mía…" In place of the name in the song, sing the name of each child in a group, one at a time, while she or he plays a small drum or stands up to dance. Children can also clap hands, snap fingers, or play their laps as drums to the rhythm of the song.

Al tam - bor, al tam - bor, al tam - bor de la_a - le -

grí - a, yo quie - ro que tú me lle - ves al tam - bor de la_a - le -

grí - a. Al tam - grí - a. Ma - rí - a, ¡oh! Ma -

rí - a Ma - rí - a, a - mi - ga mí a, yo

quie-ro que tú me lle-ves al tam-bor de la_a-le-grí-a. Al tam-

grí-a, al tam-bor de la_a-le-grí-a

CORO

Al tambor, al tambor,
al tambor de la alegría,
yo quiero que tú me lleves
al tambor de la alegría.
[cantar dos veces]

María, ¡oh! María
María, amiga mía,
yo quiero que tú me lleves
al tambor de la alegría.

CHORUS

Play the drum, play the drum,
play the drum from Panama,
come on let's play the drum
tum, tum, tum, la, la, la, la, la.
[sing twice]

María, Oh! María
María, my dear friend,
it's time to sing and dance
with the drum tum, tum, la, la, la.

Vamos a la mar · Let's Go to the Sea

This song has its origins in Guatemala. Children can also clap hands, snap fingers, click their tongues, or slap thighs in place of the "tun, tun" end-of-line rhythm.

Va-mos a la mar, tun, tun, a co-mer pes-ca-do, tun, tun,

fri-ti-to y a-sa-do, tun, tun, en sar-tén de pa-lo, tun, tun.

Vamos a la mar, tun, tun,
a comer pescado, tun, tun,
fritito y asado, tun, tun,
en sartén de palo, tun, tun.

Let's go to the sea, tun, tun,
to enjoy the best fish, tun, tun,
eat it fried or grilled, tun, tun,
in a wooden dish, tun, tun.

Vamos a la mar, tun, tun,
a comer pescado, tun, tun,
boca colorada, tun, tun,
en sartén de palo, tun, tun.

Let's go to the sea, tun, tun,
to enjoy the best fish, tun, tun,
red-mouthed fish so tasty, tun, tun,
in a wooden dish, tun, tun.

Los elefantes · The Elephant Song

This counting song can also be played as a game. While the group stands in a circle and sings, one child makes the slow-motion sway walk of an elephant inside the circle. At the end of the first verse, the child picks a second child, and both do the slow-motion elephant sway walk. Then the second child picks a third, and so on. This version of the song comes from Argentina.

Un e-le-fan-te se ba-lan-cea-ba so-bre la te-la de u-na a- ra - ña.

Co - mo ve-í - a que re-sis-tí - a fue a lla-mar a o-tro e-le-fan - te.

Un elefante se balanceaba	One elephant went out to play
sobre la tela de una araña.	out on a spider's web one day.
Como veía que resistía	He had such enormous fun
fue a llamar a otro elefante.	he called another elephant to play.
Dos elefantes se balanceaban	Two elephants went out to play
sobre la tela de una araña.	out on a spider's web one day.
Como veían que resistía	They had such enormous fun
fueron a llamar a otro elefante.	they called another elephant to play.
Tres elefantes...	Three elephants...

La granja · The Farm

This song is also sung in other Latin American countries as "Mi rancho" (My Ranch).
In Argentina it is called "La chacra" (The Farm). When singing it in a group, it's fun
for each child to be a different animal—chick, cow, pig, and so on. When the song calls
for the animal sound, the designated child makes it. Then everybody joins in on the
chorus and other verses. Notice the way different languages represent different animal
noises.

Ven - gan a ver mi gran - ja que es her - mo_____ sa. Ven - gan a ver mi

gran - ja que es her - mo_____ sa. El pa - ti - to ha - ce a -

sí, cuá, cuá. El pa - ti - to ha - ce a - sí, cuá, cuá. Oh,

ven - gan, a - mi - gos, ven - gan, a - mi - gos, ven - gan, a - mi - gos, ven - gan. Oh,

Vengan a ver mi granja
que es hermosa.   [cantar dos veces]
El patito hace así, cuá, cuá.   [dos veces]

CORO
Oh, vengan, amigos,
vengan, amigos,
vengan, amigos, vengan.   [cantar dos veces]

Come to see my farm
for it is beautiful.   [sing twice]
The duck goes like this, quack, quack.   [sing twice]

CHORUS
Oh, come, my friends,
Oh, come, my friends,
Oh, come to see my farm.   [sing twice]

Repeat the song, replacing the verse in boldface with one of the following verses.

El pollito hace así, pío, pío.
La vaquita hace así, mú, mú.
El puerquito hace así, oinc, oinc.
El burrito hace así, íja, íja.
El gallito hace así, kikiri, kí.
El perrito hace así, guau, guau.
El gatito hace así, miau, miau.

The chick goes like this, peep, peep.
The cow goes like this, moo, moo.
The pig goes like this, oink, oink.
The donkey goes like this, hee haw, hee haw.
The rooster goes like this, cock-a-doodle-doo.
The dog goes like this, bow wow.
The cat goes like this, meow, meow.

La víbora de la mar · The Sea Serpent

Many versions of this song-game can be found. Two players, children or adults, hold their hands up high to make a bridge or gate. The rest of the players form a line, holding the waist or shoulders of the person in front of them, and weave under the bridge like a sea serpent. On the last line, the bridge makers drop arms, catch a child in the sea-serpent line, and gently rock him or her back and forth. Then the song-game resumes. Several bridges or gates can be made.

A la víbora, víbora
de la mar, de la mar
por aquí pueden pasar.
Los de adelante corren mucho,
los de atrás se quedarán
tras, tras, tras, tras.

*The sea serpent we like to play
to have fun, to have fun
under the bridge all on track.
Children in front go faster and faster,
if you don't follow, you'll stay back,
back, back, back, back.*

La araña pequeñita · The Eensy, Weensy Spider

This finger-rhyme song is familiar to many children. The spider going up the water-spout is made by walking the hands, forefinger to thumb, upward. Wiggly fingers coming down make the rain, and vigorous arm gestures wash the spider out. An arm circle shows the sun, an expansive gesture dries out the rain, and the spider climbs again, forefinger to thumb. The great big spider is made with palms facing each other, one up, one down, and the arms moving apart, then together.

La a- ra-ña pe-que-ñi-ta su-bió, su-bió, su-bió. Vi-no la

llu-via y se la lle-vó. Sa-lió el sol y to-do lo se-

có, y la a-ra-ña pe-que-ñi-ta su-bió, su-bió, su-bió

La araña pequeñita	*The eensy, weensy spider*	La araña grandotota	*The great big spider*
subió, subió, subió.	*went up the waterspout.*	subió, subió, subió.	*went up the waterspout.*
Vino la lluvia	*Down came the rain*	Vino la lluvia	*Down came the rain*
y se la llevó.	*and washed the spider out.*	y se la llevó.	*and washed the spider out.*
Salió el sol	*Out came the sun*	Salió el sol	*Out came the sun*
y todo lo secó,	*and dried up all the rain,*	y todo lo secó,	*and dried up all the rain,*
y la araña pequeñita	*and the eensy, weensy spider*	y la araña grandotota	*and the great big spider*
subió, subió, subió.	*went up the spout again.*	subió, subió, subió.	*went up the spout again.*

Las mañanitas · Special Morning Song

This is a traditional Mexican song that people sing early in the morning on birthdays or on other special days. Young men also serenade their girlfriends with this beautiful song. There are many mañanitas songs—this is only one of them.

Es - tas son las ma - ña - ni - tas que can - ta - ba el rey Da - vid. Hoy que es

día de tu cum - ple_a - ños te las can - ta - mos a - sí. Des -

pier - ta, mi bien, des - pier - ta, mi - ra que ya_a - ma - ne - ció, ya los

pa - ja - ri - llos can - tan, la lu - na ya se me - tió. Des - tió.

(Lyrics on next page)

Estas son las mañanitas
que cantaba el rey David.
Hoy que es día de tu cumpleaños
te las cantamos así.

CORO
Despierta, mi bien, despierta,
mira que ya amaneció,
ya los pajarillos cantan,
la luna ya se metió.

Si el sereno de la esquina
me quisiera hacer favor
de apagar su linternita
mientras que pasa mi amor.

Despierta, mi bien…

Ahora sí, señor sereno,
le agradezco su favor,
prenda ya su linternita
que ya ha pasado mi amor.

Despierta, mi bien…

We are singing morning songs
as King David used to do.
Since today it is your birthday
we are here to sing them to you.

CHORUS
Awaken, my love, awaken,
and see that the day has dawned,
that the little birds are singing
and that the moon is long gone.

If the friendly corner watchman
might consent to be so kind
and put out his hanging lantern
as I watch my love pass by.

Awaken, my love…

It's all right now, Mr. Watchman,
thanks a lot for being so nice,
you may now relight your lantern,
my love already passed by.

Awaken, my love…

La villa · *The Village*

Here's a traditional chant a child can say when playfully taking over a seat that has been vacated. Or the rhyme can be recited as a way of asking for a seat.

El que se fué a la villa
perdió su silla.

Move your feet,
lose your seat.

OR

Left my chair to go into town,
lost my chair, I can't sit down.

Compadre, cómpreme un coco · Compadre, Buy Me a Coconut

The word *compadre* is a term of honor denoting a man who is such a good friend that he is the godfather of his friend's child. This rhyme from the Dominican Republic uses that word to make a tricky tongue twister. It can be recited accompanied by finger snapping, clapping, or striking the thighs with the palms to keep the rhythm.

Com - pa - dre, cóm - pre - me un co - co, com -

pa - dre, no com - pro co - co___ por - que co - mo po - co co - co

co - mo___ po - co co - co com - pro. Com - com - pro.

Compadre, cómpreme un coco,
compadre, no compro coco
porque como poco coco como,
poco coco compro.   [cantar dos veces]

Compadre, buy me a coconut,
compadre, I don't buy coconut.
Since I eat very little coconut,
few coconuts I buy.   [sing twice]

De colores · Bright with Colors

"De colores" came to the Americas from central Spain in the sixteenth century and is now sung all over the Spanish-speaking world on special occasions and celebrations. It is also the anthem of the United Farmworkers of America, a union founded by César Chávez, most of whose members are Spanish-speaking. People hold hands and sway while singing this beautiful song.

De_____ co - lo - res, de co - lo - res se vis - ten los

cam - pos en la pri - ma - ve - ra_____ De_____ co -

lo - res, de co - lo - res son los pa - ja - ri - tos que

vie - nen de a - fue - ra_____ De_____

(Lyrics on page 31)

De colores,
de colores se visten los campos
en la primavera.
De colores,
de colores son los pajaritos que vienen
de afuera.
De colores,
de colores es el arcoiris que vemos
lucir.

CORO
Y por eso los grandes amores
de muchos colores me gustan
a mí.   [cantar dos veces]

Canta el gallo,
canta el gallo con el kiri, kiri, kiri, kiri, kiri.
La gallina,
la gallina con el cara, cara, cara, cara, cara.
Los pollitos,
los pollitos con el pío, pío, pío, pío, pí.

CORO
Y por eso…

De colores,
bright with colors the mountains and valleys
dress up in the springtime.
De colores,
bright with colors all the little birds
fill the skies in the daytime.
De colores,
bright with colors the rainbow brings joy
with the glory of spring.

CHORUS
And a bright love with colors has found us
with peace all around us
that makes our hearts sing.   [sing twice]

Hear the rooster,
hear rooster singing kiri, kiri, kiri, kiri, kiri.
In the morning,
in the morning the hen sings her cara, cara, cara, cara, cara.
All day singing,
baby chicks all day sing pío, pío, pío, pío, pí.

CHORUS
And a bright love . . .

Los pollitos · The Baby Chicks

This Cuban version of "Los pollitos" makes a good game. For the first verse, one child represents the hen, and the rest of the children walk around the hen in a circle, moving their elbows up and down to imitate baby chicks. For the second verse, the circle stops moving and the hen walks around looking for food and feeding the chicks. For the third, the chicks sit down and close their eyes to rest, while the hen walks around giving them comfort.

Los pollitos dicen	Baby chicks are singing
"pío, pío, pío",	*"pío, pío, pío,"*
cuando tienen hambre,	*"mamma we are hungry,"*
cuando tienen frío.	*"mamma we are cold."*
La gallina busca	*Mamma looks for wheat,*
el maíz y el trigo,	*mamma looks for corn,*
les da la comida	*mamma feeds them dinner,*
y les presta abrigo.	*mamma keeps them warm.*
Bajo sus dos alas	*Under mamma's wings*
acurrucaditos	*sleeping in the hay*
hasta el otro día	*baby chicks all huddle*
duermen los pollitos.	*until the next day.*

Las hormiguitas · The Little Ants

José-Luis Orozco wrote this rhyme in California. It can be played as a lively follow-the-leader game. In a line, children follow a leader, who makes up movements to the verses of the song. Children can take turns being the leader every other verse or so.

Por los ce - rri - tos _____ y ve - re - di - tas _____ van ca - mi - nan - do _____ las hor - mi - gui - tas _____

Por los cerritos	*Over the little hills*
y vereditas	*and all the little roads*
van caminando	*the line of little ants*
las hormiguitas.	***walks on and on.***
Las hormiguitas,	*The line of little ants,*
las hormiguitas,	*the line of little ants,*
van caminando	*the line of little ants*
las hormiguitas.	***walks on and on.***

Repeat the song, each time replacing the words in boldface with one of the phrases below.

van de puntitas	*walks on tippy-toes*
van dando vueltas	*spins on and on*
saltan y saltan	*jumps on and on*
bailan y bailan	*dances on and on*
van patinando	*skates on and on*
ya se despiden	*all waves good-bye*

Sana, sana · Sana, Sana

This rhyme has magical healing power. Gently rub your fingers over a cut, bruise, or other injury in a circular motion, reciting the rhyme several times. The injured person will quickly feel better. "Sana, sana" means "heal, heal." This version comes from Ecuador. Use the rhythm below when reciting "Sana, sana."

Sa - na, | sa - na co - li - ta de | ra - na, si no sa - nas | hoy sa - na - rás ma - | ña - na.

Sana, sana
colita de rana,
si no sanas hoy
sanarás mañana.

Sana, sana
frog tail is in sorrow.
If I rub today
you'll be healed tomorrow.

Un ratoncito · A Little Mouse

This is a traditional rhyme. Walk your forefinger and middle finger over your opposite arm—or someone else's arm—from hand to elbow. This is un ratoncito, "a little mouse." Clap once before you say the last line.

Un ratoncito
iba por un arado
y este cuentecito
ya se ha acabado.

A little mouse ran
to swim in a pond
and this little story
is now long gone.

Cuatro camaroncitos · Four Little Shrimp

This nonsense song from Nicaragua can be acted out by children any way they like. They can pretend to be swimming underwater, or serving coffee, or whatever they wish.

A - llá en los ma - res don - de yo es - tu - ve den - tro del a - gua cer - ca de un mes ___ ha - bía u - nos pe - ces tan chi - qui - ti - tos co - mo la pun - ta de un al - fi -

ler. Cua - tro ca - ma - ron - ci - tos me da - ban de co -

mer ___ y u - na sar - di - na gran - de me ser - ví - a el ca - fé.

Allá en los mares
donde yo estuve
dentro del agua
cerca de un mes,
había unos peces
tan chiquititos
como la punta
de un alfiler.

There in the ocean
where I was living
under the water
close to a month,
the fish were tiny
so very tiny
just like the point
of a little pin.

Cuatro camaroncitos
me daban de comer,
y una sardina grande
me servía el café.

Four teeny-weeny-wee shrimp
fed me all dressed in pink,
and a humongous sardine
was serving coffee to drink.

¡Ay! cómo me quemaba,
agua por Dios pedía,
y un camarón me dijo,
"Eso sí que no hay aquí".

Oh boy the coffee was hot!
Water for burns I ordered,
and the silly shrimp responded,
"Sorry there's no water here."

El burrito enfermo · The Sick Little Donkey

This cumulative song is popular all over Latin America. Singers can alternate clapping their hands with stamping their feet at the "tap, tap, tap, tap" end of every verse. In English, you can also add the word "Hooray!" Children can point to the different parts of their bodies and pretend to put on the clothing mentioned in the song. Or one child can be the sick little donkey, and others can take turns bringing the donkey remedies.

A mi bu - rro, a mi bu - rro le due - le la ca - be - za, y el

mé - di - co le man - da u - na go - rri - ta ne - gra, u - na go - rri - ta

ne - gra y mue - ve las pa - ti - tas tap, tap, tap, tap.

A mi burro, a mi burro
le duele la cabeza,
y el médico le manda
una gorrita negra,
una gorrita negra
y mueve las patitas
tap, tap, tap, tap.

My donkey has a headache,
my donkey cannot play,
the vet will soon deliver
a black hat and some hay,
a black hat and some hay,
and click your little hooves
tap, tap, tap, tap. Hooray!

(Lyrics continued on next page)

A mi burro, a mi burro
le duele la garganta,
y el médico le manda
una bufanda blanca,
una bufanda blanca,
una gorrita negra
y mueve las patitas
tap, tap, tap, tap.

My donkey has a sore throat,
my donkey cannot play,
the vet will soon deliver
a white scarf and some hay,
a white scarf and some hay,
a black hat for the headache,
and click your little hooves
tap, tap, tap, tap. Hooray!

A mi burro, a mi burro
le duelen las costillas,
y el médico le manda
chaqueta amarilla,
chaqueta amarilla,
una bufanda blanca,
una gorrita negra
y mueve las patitas
tap, tap, tap, tap.

My donkey's ribs are very sore,
my donkey cannot play,
the vet will soon deliver
a yellow coat and hay,
a yellow coat and hay,
a white scarf for the sore throat,
a black hat for the headache,
and click your little hooves
tap, tap, tap, tap. Hooray!

A mi burro, a mi burro
le duele el corazón,
y el médico le manda
gotitas de limón,
gotitas de limón,
chaqueta amarilla,
una bufanda blanca,
una gorrita negra
y mueve las patitas
tap, tap, tap, tap.

My donkey's heart is aching,
my donkey cannot play,
the vet will soon deliver
lemon drops and hay,
lemon drops and hay,
a yellow coat for sore ribs,
a white scarf for the sore throat,
a black hat for the headache,
and click your little hooves
tap, tap, tap, tap. Hooray!

A mi burro, a mi burro
ya no le duele nada,
y el médico le manda
trocitos de manzana,
trocitos de manzana,
gotitas de limón,
chaqueta amarilla,
una bufanda blanca,
una gorrita negra
y mueve las patitas
tap, tap, tap, tap.

My donkey is very happy,
my donkey can now play,
the vet will soon deliver
green apples and some hay,
green apples and some hay,
lemon drops for heartache,
a yellow coat for sore ribs,
a white scarf for the sore throat,
a black hat for the headache,
and click your little hooves
tap, tap, tap, tap. Hooray!

Caballito blanco · My Little White Horse

This version of "Caballito blanco" comes from Chile. Singing this song, children can pretend to ride horses (or use brooms or sticks as horses), clicking their tongues before and after the song in a trotting rhythm.

Ca - ba - lli - to blan - co, sá - ca - me de a - quí ____

llé - va - me_a mi pue - blo don - de yo na - cí.

Caballito blanco,
sácame de aquí,
llévame a mi pueblo
donde yo nací.

Tengo, tengo, tengo,
tú no tienes nada,
tengo tres ovejas
en una cabaña.

Una me da leche,
otra me da lana,
y otra mantequilla
para la semana.

My little white horse,
take me now to my home,
take me to the nice town
where I was born.

I am very glad,
I am very lucky,
for I have three lambs
that make me so happy.

One lamb gives me wool,
one lamb gives me milk,
one lamb gives me butter
every single week.

La piñata · The Piñata

These are only a few of the many verses from two traditional Mexican songs that are sung during special celebrations like Christmas, Las Posadas, or school and birthday parties. A piñata is a clay pot or papier-mâché figure covered with colorful paper and filled with sweets and/or toys. A child is usually blindfolded and given a stick with which to try to break the piñata and spill out the goodies inside. Everybody shares the presents and helps clean up afterward!

An - da - le a - mi - go, no te di - la - tes con la ca -
nas - ta de los ca - ca - hua - tes. An - da - le a - ci - ón.

Da - le, da - le, da - le, no pier - das el ti - no,

mi - de la dis - tan - cia que hay en el ca - mi - no.

Andale amigo, no te dilates
con la canasta de los cacahuates.

Andale amigo, sal del rincón
con la canasta de la colación.

No quiero oro, ni quiero plata,
yo lo que quiero es romper la piñata.

Dale, dale, dale,
no pierdas el tino,
mide la distancia
que hay en el camino.

Bring the piñata with no delay,
we want to party, we want to play.

Come on my friend, please don't be tardy,
bring us the baskets with all the candy.

I don't want silver, gold doesn't matter,
all that I want is to break the piñata.

Hit, hit the piñata,
do not lose your aim,
measure well the distance
or you'll lose the way.

Repeat the last stanza, substituting the following lines for the last two lines in boldface.

porque si lo pierdes
pierdes el camino.

because if you lose it
you will lose the way.

Nochebuena · Christmas Eve

"Nochebuena" is a Mexican song that celebrates Christmas Eve. The buñuelos mentioned in the song are Mexican pastries that are made of flour dough, deep fried, then covered with honey or syrup and sprinkled with cinnamon powder. Mmm…delicious!

Es-ta | no-che es No-che - bue-na, | no-che de co-mer bu - ñue-los,

no-che de lu - na, | no-che de es tre - llas | pa-ra los ni - ños | bue - nos.

Esta noche es Nochebuena,	*Tonight is Christmas Eve,*
noche de comer buñuelos,	*a good night to eat buñuelos,*
noche de luna,	*night with a big moon,*
noche de estrellas	*night with bright stars,*
para los niños buenos.	*night for all the children.*
Esta noche es Nochebuena,	*Tonight is Christmas Eve,*
noche de comer buñuelos,	*a good night to eat buñuelos,*
noche de luna,	*night with a big moon,*
noche de estrellas	*night with bright stars,*
para las niñas buenas.	*night for all the children.*

Nanita, nana · Nanita, Nana

"Nanita, nana" is sung at Christmastime in many Spanish-speaking countries. It's also sung as a lullaby. "Nanita" is an affectionate way of referring to a "nana," a baby-sitter or nanny.

A la na-ni-ta, na - na, na-ni-ta, na - na, na-ni-ta, e - a,

mi Je-sús tie-ne sue - ño, ben-di - to se - a, ben-di-to se - a.

Pa-ja-ri-llo que can-tas____ so - bre el al - men-dro____

no des-pier-tes al ni - ño____ que es____ tá dur - mien-do

A la nanita, nana,
nanita, nana, nanita, ea,
mi Jesús tiene sueño,
bendito sea, bendito sea. *[cantar dos veces]*

Pajarillo que cantas
sobre el almendro,
no despiertes al niño
que está durmiendo.

Duerme mientras la cuna
lo balancea
a la nanita, nana,
nanita, ea.

*Nana, nanita, nana,
nanita, nana, nanita, eh-a,
baby Jesus is sleeping,
blessings for him, nanita, eh-a.* *[sing twice]*

*Little bird that is singing
on the almond tree,
please don't wake up the baby,
he's soundly asleep.*

*He's sleeping while the cradle
rocks, to and fro,
nana, nanita, nana,
nanita, eh-a.*

Naranja dulce · Sweet Orange

This farewell song is sung throughout Latin America. It can also be played as a game. For the first verse, children hold hands and walk around a child in the center of the circle. For the second verse, the circle stops moving and the center child picks another for handshaking and a farewell hug. For the third verse, the first child joins the circle, waving good-bye to the second child, who stays in the center. The game continues this way.

Na - ran - ja dul - ce, li - món par - ti - do, da - me un a -

bra - zo que yo te pi - do.

Naranja dulce,	*Sweet honey orange,*
limón partido,	*a slice of lemon, dear,*
dame un abrazo	*if I could hug you,*
que yo te pido.	*if I could have you near.*
Si fueran falsos	*Time to shake hands now,*
mis juramentos,	*a hug for farewell,*
en otros tiempos	*Adiós amigo(a),*
se olvidaran.	*I wish you well.*
Toca la marcha,	*The march is playing,*
mi pecho llora,	*I'll part tomorrow,*
adiós señora,	*Good-bye my dear friend,*
yo ya me voy.	*I leave with sorrow.*

El coquí · Coquí, the Little Frog

For many years a type of little frog in Puerto Rico has delighted children and grown-ups with its delightful song—"coquí, coquí." The sound has given the frog its name.

El co - quí, el co - quí a mí me en - can - ta, es tan lin-do el can -

tar del___ co - quí_____ Por las no - ches al ir a a-cos -

tar - me_____ me a - dor - me - ce can - tan - do a - sí. Co -

quí, co - quí, co - quí, quí, quí, quí. Co - quí_____

El coquí, el coquí, a mí me encanta,
es tan lindo el cantar del coquí.
Por las noches al ir a acostarme,
me adormece cantando así.

Coquí, coquí, coquí, quí, quí, quí.
[cantar dos veces]

My *coquí*, little frog, how I love you,
for your songs give me comfort and peace.
Every night I can go to sleep happy
when I hear lullabies from *coquí*.

Coquí, coquí, coquí, quí, quí, quí.
[sing twice]

Paz y libertad · Peace and Liberty

This is an original song by José-Luis Orozco. It can be sung any time of the year, including Christmas. Children hold hands while they sing the song.

Lento

Pa-ra los ni-ños de to-do el mun-do que-re-mos paz y li-ber-

1. C — tad._____ Pa-ra los
2. C — tad.
% C — Paz_____ que-re-mos paz

_____ y li-ber-tad_____ en es-te mun-

1. — do.
2. — do. Ya no más ham-

Para los niños de todo el mundo
queremos paz y libertad.   [cantar dos veces]

CORO
Paz, queremos paz
y libertad en este mundo.   [cantar dos veces]

Ya no más hambre, ya no más guerra,
queremos paz en esta tierra.   [dos veces]

Paz, queremos paz...

Para los pobres y los viejitos
queremos paz y libertad.   [dos veces]

Paz, queremos paz...

Ya no más bombas ni radiación,
no más ideas de exterminación.   [dos veces]

Paz, queremos paz...

For all the children in the world
we want peace and liberty.   [sing twice]

CHORUS
Peace, we all want peace
and liberty in this world.   [sing twice]

No more hunger, no more war,
we want peace on this earth.   [twice]

Peace, we all want peace...

For the poor and the elderly
we want peace and liberty.   [twice]

Peace, we all want peace...

No more bombs, no more radiation,
no more ideas of extermination.   [twice]

Peace, we all want peace...

Duérmete, mi niño · Go to Sleep, My Baby

This lullaby originated in Spain and is sung throughout Latin America. For generations, mothers have used it to transmit love, warmth, and peace to their children as they fall asleep.

Duér-me-te, mi ni - ño, duér-me-te so - li - to,

que cuan-do des - pier - tes te da - ré a - to - li - to.

Duérmete, mi niño,	*Go to sleep, my baby,*	Duérmete, mi niña,	*Go to sleep, my baby,*
duérmete solito,	*sleep in peace and dream,*	duérmete, mi sol,	*go to sleep, my love,*
que cuando despiertes	*for when you awaken*	duérmete pedazo	*go to sleep, my sweetheart,*
te daré atolito.	*I will give you cream.*	de mi corazón.	*go to sleep, my dove.*

Subject Index